This book belongs to.

....

....

age ....

First published in Great Britain 2003
This edition reissued 2007 by Egmont UK Limited
239 Kensington High Street, London W8 6SA

ISBN 978 0 6035 6305 8
1 3 5 7 9 10 8 6 4 2
Printed in China

Contents

Thomas, Percy and
the Squeak
pages 3-15

Twin Trouble
pages 17-29

Thomas, James and
the Red Balloon
pages 31-43

Harvey to the Rescue
pages 45-57

Thomas, Percy and the Squeak

The engines were very excited. A famous singer called Allicia Botti was coming to sing at a concert. All the engines wanted to collect her from the Docks.

"I will be chosen to collect her," said James. "I'm the shiniest."
"But I'm the most important," huffed Gordon.
Thomas wanted to feel important, too.

Percy pulled up next to Gordon. His face was very grimy. "The Fat Controller certainly won't choose dirty Percy," laughed Gordon.

The Fat Controller didn't choose James and he didn't choose Gordon. He chose Thomas!

"Make sure you are squeaky clean," said The Fat Controller. "Yes, Sir," said Thomas, proudly.

Thomas went to be washed. Percy was waiting, too. "Move over," said Thomas, rudely. "I'm the important engine today!"

"But I need a wash," wailed Percy. "My passengers will laugh at me!"
"I need to be squeaky clean," said Thomas. "So you'll have to wait."
Percy chuffed away, still very dirty.

Thomas was shiny and clean. But as he was coupled to Annie and Clarabel, he heard a strange squeaking noise. His Driver oiled Annie and Clarabel's wheels. "That should stop the squeak," he said.

As Thomas passed Percy, he heard the squeaking noise again. "Is everything all right?" asked Percy. "Erm, yes, everything's fine," said Thomas.

As he passed a lighthouse, Thomas heard the squeak again! He was worried. What was making that noise? He hoped it would stop before he reached the Docks.

But the noise didn't stop. Thomas squeaked into the Docks, where the singer was waiting. He hoped she would not notice the noise.

The Fat Controller opened the door for Allicia Botti to climb aboard.

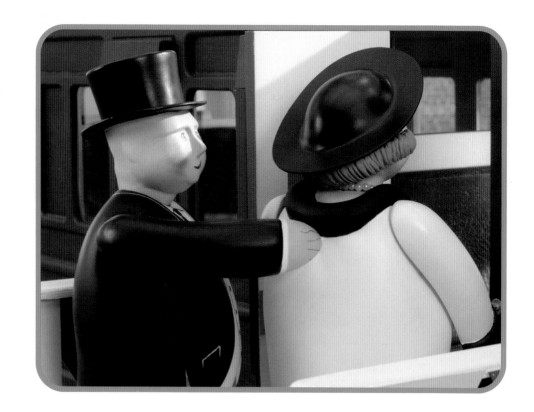

But when she looked into the carriage, Allicia Botti saw a little mouse! "Squeak!" said the mouse.

Allicia Botti screamed and screamed. "I can't travel in trains full of mice!" she said.

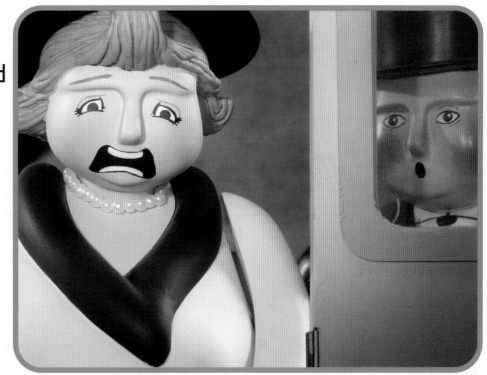

The Fat Controller was very embarrassed. Thomas didn't feel important any more.

Just then, Percy chuffed up. He looked dirtier than ever. "What a lovely engine!" said Allicia Botti. "All dirty like a proper steam engine. I want him to take me to the concert."

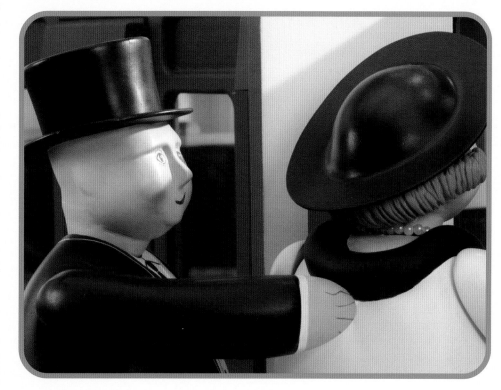

So Allicia boarded the train and Percy steamed away. He felt very proud.

Later, Thomas saw Percy at the water tower.
"I'm sorry I was so rude to you earlier," he said.
"It's good to be friends again," said Percy.

"What happened to your mouse?" asked Percy.

Thomas smiled. "Come with me and I'll show you," he said.

The Fat Controller had made the little mouse her very own home in the corner of the station. And Thomas had named her Allicia!

Twin Trouble

Donald and Douglas were Scottish engines. They were twins and they nearly always worked together.

One day, they were working hard, pulling a heavy load through the countryside.

Further down the track, Trevor the Traction engine was pulling a cart-load of hay. Suddenly, one of his wheels broke. It fell off on to the track! Donald and Douglas were approaching.

"Oh, no!" cried Trevor. He knew there would be an accident.

Donald saw the wheel and tried to brake in time. "Stop!" he cried, but the Troublesome Trucks pushed him on. Donald crashed off the tracks and was covered in hay.

"You need a haircut!" laughed Douglas. Donald didn't think it was very funny, but he laughed when the wind blew the hay on to Douglas! Now Douglas was cross.

Before long, the twins were hardly speaking to one another. They even refused to look at each other.
The next day, The Fat Controller wanted an engine to help Duck at the power plant.

"May I go, Sir?" asked Donald.
"I only need one engine," said The Fat Controller, "not both of you."
"I am one engine," said Donald. "I don't want to work with Douglas."
The Fat Controller was surprised, but he agreed.

Thomas was worried. "Won't you miss each other?" he asked. "I'll work much better on my own," said Douglas. "I'm off!" said Donald.

So Donald started working with Duck. He enjoyed taking coal trucks along the coastal track.

But then things started to go wrong.

"Did you shunt those trucks on to the other line?" asked Donald.

"You said you wanted them on the other line," Duck replied.

"I didn't mean that line, I meant the *other* line," said Donald.

"Douglas would have known what I meant," he added.

Meanwhile, Douglas was working on his own.

He thought the Island of Sodor looked beautiful, but he was sad because he had no one to share it with.

Although he tried hard not to, Douglas was beginning to miss his twin. He decided that he would speak to Donald that night.

"Have you come to say you are sorry?" said Donald.
This made Douglas very cross.
"I've nothing to be sorry for!" he said and steamed away in a huff.

The next day, Donald was in a bad mood. He wasn't looking at what he was doing. Duck saw that he was too close to the buffers. "Whoa!" he said.

But Donald thought Duck had said 'Go', so he rolled back and crashed into the buffers.

Duck was shocked. "What were you thinking?" he said. "This would never have happened if you were working with Douglas," said Donald's Driver, crossly.

Duck couldn't pull Donald back on to the rails, so he went to get some help.

"Donald's in trouble!" Duck said to Douglas. "Oh, no!" cried Douglas. "I'm on my way!"
And he steamed out of the depot as fast as he could.

Douglas gently pulled Donald back on to the track. "Thank you," said Donald. "And I'm really sorry!"
"Yes, I'm sorry, too!" said Douglas.
"Good! I'm glad you're friends again!" said Duck.

From then on, Donald and Douglas always worked well together and they never argued – well, hardly ever!

Thomas, James
and the Red Balloon

One day, The Fat Controller sent Thomas to take something very important to the airfield.

"What have you got there?" asked Percy. "It's a balloon," said Thomas. "A very special balloon."

Thomas soon arrived at the airfield. People were waiting there to help unload the balloon.

Hot air was pumped into the balloon. As if by magic, the balloon rose silently into the sky. Everyone was very impressed.

Just then, James arrived.
"What is that?" he said, when he saw the balloon.
"It's a hot air balloon," said Thomas.
"Holidaymakers can ride in it."

"But what if it takes our passengers away?" said James. This made Thomas very worried.

The balloon could be seen by everyone on the Island, as it floated up high in the sky.

It took people on trips all over the Island. James did not like it.
"Passengers belong on trains, not in balloons," he said.

After that, wherever James went on the Island, he saw the red balloon.

And Thomas and James often had to take passengers to the airfield, so they could go for a ride in the balloon.

James had had enough!
"Those people shouldn't be travelling by balloon," he said. "Rails are better than hot air any day!"

One day, Thomas and James were at a level crossing when the balloon came drifting towards them.
"Help! We're out of hot air!" said the balloon Driver.

The balloon landed on top of James! He was scared, so he let out a huge burst of steam. Whoosh! The balloon rose up into the air again.

"Well done, James," said The Fat Controller. "Your hot air rescued the balloon."

"I wish it hadn't," said James. "Now our passengers will all ride in the balloon instead."

The Fat Controller laughed. "Don't worry, the holidaymakers all need a lift to and from the airfield by train!"

James was delighted.

The Fat Controller was right. The engines were busier than ever, taking passengers to and from the airfield.

Thomas and Bertie often had races to see who could get to the airfield first.

All the engines started looking out for the balloon. One day, Henry was surprised to see it floating above him by the beach.

Donald and Douglas thought the balloon was splendid. They liked watching it float over the engine sheds.

Now, whenever James sees the balloon, he whistles and toots at it.

And sometimes, when James is asleep at night, he has pleasant dreams . . .

. . . of the red balloon floating in the sky!

Harvey to the Rescue

All the engines love working at the Docks. There's always lots of work to do, and they like seeing all the new arrivals on the Island of Sodor.

One day, Cranky was unloading a new engine. It was very heavy. "This makes my chin ache," said Cranky, crossly.

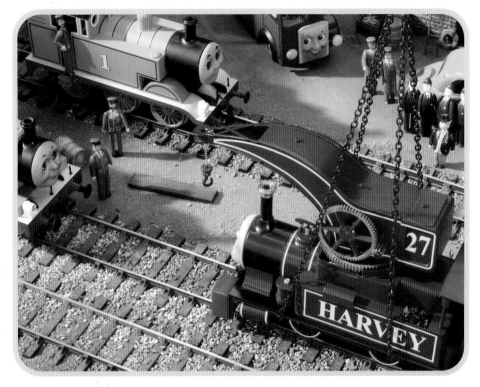

"This is Harvey, a crane engine," said The Fat Controller. Harvey was glad to be on the ground again. He had not liked being up in the air, dangling from Cranky's arm.

The Gentlemen from the Railway Board had come to visit. They were going to see Harvey doing a demonstration, so they should decide if he could join the Railway.

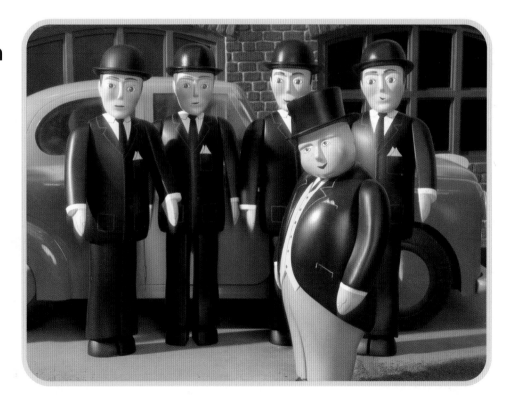

"What's a demonstration?" asked Percy.

"It's when you show off what you can do," said Thomas.

"Like when Thomas and I have a race," said Bertie.

"Vrooooomm! Vrooooomm!"

That night, Thomas saw Harvey by the engine sheds. He looked sad. The other engines were talking about him.

"Harvey's different!" said Henry.
"He doesn't even look like an engine!" said Gordon.
"He's just Cranky on wheels," said James.

"He's not carrying my mail," said Percy. Poor Harvey. No one wanted to be his friend.

Thomas felt sorry for Harvey. "Don't worry," he said to him. "It takes time to make new friends." But Harvey wasn't sure he wanted to stay where no one wanted him.

The next morning, Harvey spoke to The Fat Controller. "The engines don't like me, Sir," he said. "I'm too different."

"Being different is what makes you special," said The Fat Controller. That made Harvey feel a little better.

Bertie was going to take the Gentlemen from the Railway Board on a tour of the Island.

Bertie felt very proud to be carrying such important passengers.

On the branch line, Percy's naughty trucks were making him go too fast. "Faster we go. Faster we go!" they cried. "Help!" cried Percy as he tried to slow down.

Percy's Driver applied the brakes, but it was too late. Percy came off the track and his trucks crashed down on to the road!

Percy's trucks had fallen on to the road in front of Bertie. "You should be more careful, Percy!" said Bertie. "Your trucks have blocked the road."

When The Fat Controller heard about the crash, he went to see Harvey. "I need you to rescue Percy and some trucks," he said. "I'll do my best, Sir," said Harvey.

Harvey worked very hard. Before long, he had lifted Percy and the trucks back on to the track.

"Thank you so much," said Percy to Harvey. "I can see now that you are a Really Useful Engine. I can't wait to tell the other engines about how you rescued me!"

The Gentlemen from the Railway Board were impressed, too. "That was the best demonstration of all!" they said. "Harvey can join the Railway." "Thank you," said Harvey, happily.

That night, the engines were talking about Harvey again. But this time it was different.
"Well done, Harvey," said Gordon.
"You're Really Useful," said James. "Welcome to the Railway!"

From that day on, Harvey worked at The Fat Controller's station and he enjoyed working with all his new engine friends.